TRYING AGAIN

By EMILY ARROW
Illustrations by KAYLA STARK
Music by EMILY ARROW

CANTATA
LEARNING

WWW.CANTATALEARNING.COM

CANTATA LEARNING

Published by Cantata Learning
1710 Roe Crest Drive
North Mankato, MN 56003
www.cantatalearning.com

Library of Congress Cataloging-in-Publication Data
Names: Arrow, Emily, author. | Stark, Kayla, illustrator.
Title: Trying again / by Emily Arrow ; illustrated by Kayla Stark ; music by Emily Arrow.
Description: North Mankato, MN : Cantata Learning, [2020] | Series: My
   feelings, my choices | Includes bibliographical references.
Identifiers: LCCN 2018053381 (print) | LCCN 2018055663 (ebook) | ISBN
   9781684104222 (eBook) | ISBN 9781684104079 (hardcover) | ISBN
   9781684104345 (pbk.)
Subjects: LCSH: Achievement motivation in children--Juvenile literature. |
   Motivation (Psychology) in children--Juvenile literature.
Classification: LCC BF723.M56 (ebook) | LCC BF723.M56 A77 2020 (print) | DDC
   155.4/138--dc23
LC record available at https://lccn.loc.gov/2018053381

Book design and art direction: Tim Palin Creative
Editorial direction: Kellie M. Hultgren
Music direction: Elizabeth Draper
Music composed and produced by Emily Arrow

Printed in the United States of America.
0406

ACCESS THE MUSIC!
SCAN CODE WITH MOBILE APP
CANTATALEARNING.COM

TIPS TO SUPPORT LITERACY AT HOME

WHY READING AND SINGING WITH YOUR CHILD IS SO IMPORTANT

Daily reading with your child leads to increased academic achievement. Music and songs, specifically rhyming songs, are a fun and easy way to build early literacy and language development. Music skills correlate significantly with both phonological awareness and reading development. Singing helps build vocabulary and speech development. And reading and appreciating music together is a wonderful way to strengthen your relationship.

READ AND SING EVERY DAY!

TIPS FOR USING CANTATA LEARNING BOOKS AND SONGS DURING YOUR DAILY STORY TIME

1. As you sing and read, point out the different words on the page that rhyme. Suggest other words that rhyme.

2. Memorize simple rhymes such as Itsy Bitsy Spider and sing them together. This encourages comprehension skills and early literacy skills.

3. Use the questions in the back of each book to guide your singing and storytelling.

4. Read the included sheet music with your child while you listen to the song. How do the music notes correlate to the words of the song?

5. Sing along on the go and at home. Access music by scanning the QR code on each Cantata book. You can also stream or download the music for free to your computer, smartphone, or mobile device.

Devoting time to daily reading shows that you are available for your child. Together, you are building language, literacy, and listening skills.

Have fun reading and singing!

Have you ever tried something that didn't work? Maybe you started making something, but it broke. Maybe you needed to learn something new before you could finish. Or maybe you just made a **mistake**. Did you feel like giving up? Or did you try again and succeed? Whether you're growing a plant or learning to ride a skateboard, trying again is how we can learn new things and **challenge** ourselves.

Are you ready to try again? Turn the page to find out and sing along!

My very own plant
is so much fun.

But, oh no, I gave it too much sun.
Oh no, I gave it too much sun.

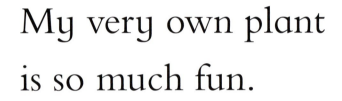

And when I think I can't,
I just add "yet."

I just can't do it . . . yet!
It isn't working . . . yet!
It isn't growing . . . yet!
But I'll still grow if I try again.

I'll water my plant
to help it grow.

But, oh no, it **overflowed**.
Oh no, it overflowed.

And when I think I can't,
I just add "yet."

I just can't do it . . . yet!
It isn't working . . . yet!
It isn't growing . . . yet!
But I'll still grow if I try again.

I can sing it a song
or take it for a ride.

But, oh no, I broke it this time.
Oh no, I broke it this time.

Everybody hits a few bumps in the road.

But don't **quit** then: try again!

Because that is when
we really grow and grow, grow and grow.

16

So when I think I can't,
I just add "yet."

I just can't do it . . . yet!
It isn't working . . . yet!
It isn't growing . . . yet!
But I'll still grow if I try again.

I'll still grow if I try again.

I'm going to try, try, try again.

20

SONG LYRICS
Trying Again

My very own plant
is so much fun.
But, oh no, I gave it too much sun.
Oh no, I gave it too much sun.

And when I think I can't,
I just add "yet."
I just can't do it . . . yet!
It isn't working . . . yet!
It isn't growing . . . yet!
But I'll still grow if I try again.

I'll water my plant
to help it grow.
But, oh no, it overflowed.
Oh no, it overflowed.

And when I think I can't,
I just add "yet."
I just can't do it . . . yet!
It isn't working . . . yet!
It isn't growing . . . yet!
But I'll still grow if I try again.

I can sing it a song
or take it for a ride.
But, oh no, I broke it this time.
Oh no, I broke it this time.

Everybody hits a few bumps in the road.
But don't quit then: try again!
Because that is when
we really grow and grow, grow and grow.

So when I think I can't,
I just add "yet."
I just can't do it . . . yet!
It isn't working . . . yet!
It isn't growing . . . yet!
But I'll still grow if I try again.

I'll still grow if I try again.
I'm going to try, try, try again.

Trying Again

Kindie
Emily Arrow

Verse

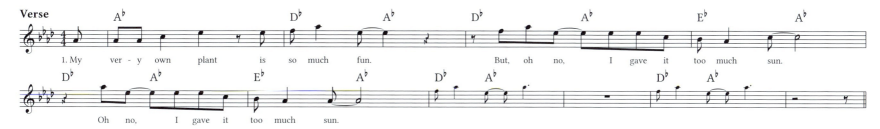

1. My ver - y own plant is so much fun. But, oh no, I gave it too much sun.

Oh no, I gave it too much sun.

Chorus

And when I think I can't, I just add "yet." I just can't do it . . . yet! It is - n't work - ing . . . yet! It

is - n't grow - ing . . . yet! But I'll still grow if I try a - gain.

I'll still grow if I try a - gain. I'm going to try, try, try a - gain.

Verse 2
I'll water my plant
to help it grow.
But, oh no, it overflowed.
Oh no, it overflowed.

Verse 3
I can sing it a song
or take it for a ride.
But, oh no, I broke it this time.
Oh no, I broke it this time.

Chorus

Bridge

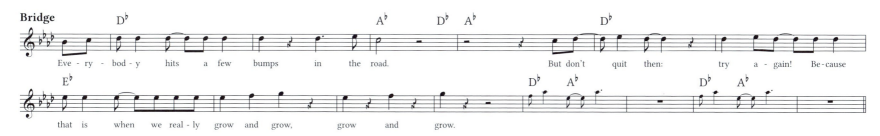

Eve - ry - bod - y hits a few bumps in the road. But don't quit then: try a - gain! Be - cause

that is when we real - ly grow and grow, grow and grow.

Chorus

GLOSSARY

challenge—get excited about trying something new, even if it will not be easy

mistake—a wrong move or decision

overflowed—filled up until it spilled over

quit—to give up

CRITICAL THINKING QUESTIONS

1. When we feel like giving up, we might say things like "I can't do it" or "It won't work." What word in the song reminds us to try again?

2. Write a letter to the character in the book asking her to try again, even when she feels like quitting. Do you think these same words could help you when you feel like giving up?

3. Name a time when you wanted to give up. What were you trying to do? Why wasn't it working? What happened? Draw a picture of how you might try it again.

TO LEARN MORE

Amstutz, Lisa J. *Creative Gardening: Growing Plants Upside Down, In Water, and More.* North Mankato, MN: Capstone, 2016.

Brown, Peter. *The Curious Garden.* New York: Little, Brown Books for Young Readers, 2009.

Petty, Dev. *Claymates.* New York: Little, Brown Books for Young Readers, 2017.

Reynolds, Peter H. *The Dot.* Cambridge, MA: Candlewick, 2003.

Stockland, Patricia M. *Debugging: You Can Fix It!* North Mankato, MN: Cantata Learning, 2018.